About the Author

After leading a very active professional life, it was important for me to continue to follow my heart in terms of what to do in the next phase of life in retirement. I hadn't written for pleasure since I was a teenager. I did begin writing in high school and continued a small amount while at home raising my children. I am using the pen name, Mikkie Bjornson, in reference to my Icelandic heritage.

Hjortur's Faery

Mikkie Bjornson

Hjortur's Faery

Olympia Publishers
London

www.olympiapublishers.com
OLYMPIA PAPERBACK EDITION

A CIP catalogue record for this title is available from the British
Library.

ISBN: 978-1-80074-371-7

This is a work of fiction. Names, characters, places and incidents
originate from the writer's experiences and imagination. Any
resemblance to actual persons, living or dead may be factual, or
not. The author has taken liberties with memories and embellished
those memories as she saw fit.

First Published in 2022

Olympia Publishers
Tallis House
2 Tallis Street
London
EC4Y 0AB
Printed in Great Britain

Dedication

This tale is dedicated to my family. With a special thanks to my granddaughter for reminding me about my faery friend and encouraging me to write about her.

Acknowledgements

Thank you to my husband, Keith, and my children, Andrew, Erin and James who encouraged me to finish this book and to see it published.

Epilogue
Iceland — 1912

Vilborg thrashed about in a sleepy fog. Something was disturbing her night. Anguish abounded. *"There is such fear and hopelessness for the people of Iceland,"* she thought in her mind. She had fallen asleep reading from the poems of Hannes Hafstein and now awoke with a start. Storm. So much power she pondered. Vilborg drifted off again into a deep sleep and woke refreshed. Her mind had cleared and ideas were flying about inside her.

So many children and families have been torn apart by the ravages of disease. "There must be something that the country can do," thought Vilborg. Vilborg was a sturdy woman of strong character. Her prominent cheekbones and thick, wavy blonde hair spoke to her Icelandic heritage. She had laid awake most of this past night struggling with the knowledge that so many of her people were struggling with disease. She was in great physical health and believed that she was in a position to do good for those experiencing tragedy.

Vilborg worked as a housemaid for Hannes Hafstein. He was a man of character who believed strongly in women's rights and the right to vote. Hannes was the current President of Iceland and a dear and kind man. He had studied abroad and was an accomplished poet. Vilborg's favorite poem written by Hannes Hafstein was 'Storm'. It spoke to love of country and emotional power within.

Vilborg really enjoyed the passionate discussions that erupted at the breakfast table in the Hafstein household. Women were encouraged to speak their minds. Along with his wife and daughters, Hannes' mother and mother-in-law lived in the house. Even as the hired help, Vilborg was cajoled into speaking her mind and voicing her opinion. Such discussions thrilled her. She so enjoyed being part of the banter.

Just yesterday, the women were discussing yet more families torn apart by illness and death. It was such a shame. So many youngsters left without mothers. Surely, she could do something to strengthen the bond between broken families and neighbours. The country was reeling from the sheer volume of tragedy.

As she always did in times of conflict within herself, Vilborg reached out to visit with her childhood faery bosom friend, Shelley. That very morning, Vilborg set up to meet with Shelley. They met at the edge of mountains where the sparseness of the rock blended into the bog. Here the ladies sat and commiserated over hot tea. It is a well-known fact in Iceland that faeries are relatives to the hidden people. Hidden people are to be taken seriously as they have much to offer to the Icelanders in respect to life and death. After all, hidden people live far longer lives that do mortal Icelanders.

Vilborg was not at all embarrassed to be seeking advice and direction from a faery. It was in Vilborg's mind that it was her responsibility to consider every option in coming up with a plan to assist her countrymen on the road to recovery from such a devastating disease.

Icelanders are a tough bunch. And they have been through so very much with the volcanic eruptions, earthquakes, drought and volcanic dust that has destroyed so many of the farms in Iceland.

Vilborg and Shelly discussed many ideas and finally Shelley yelled out, "I have the perfect idea! "Many of our young faeries are finding it difficult to strike up conversations with the young folk of today. They are finding the youngsters do not believe in them as their parents did. A good part of a faery's upbringing includes community work and these youngsters are missing out on friendships that last more than a lifetime. Perhaps we could encourage younger faeries to try again to befriend a young child that has lost a parent or a loved one?"

Vilborg grinned and felt the beginnings of a plan. "Mr Hafstein is planning a trip abroad. I will need to meet with him straight away to see if he would be in agreement with our plan. Perhaps he will agree to call together all of the regional members of parliament to meet with the elders of the hidden folk and the older faeries at Pingfella" for old times' sake."

"Shelley, if I can persuade Mr Halfstein to support our plan, can you call together your people and have them meet at Pingfella?" asked Vilborg.

Both ladies beamed with anticipation at the thought of a plan that might assist the country to get back on its feet.

After a deep embrace, the ladies parted company and

set about to engage in conversations for attendance at this parliamentary summons that was to change lives.

Hannes Hafstein was President of Iceland and took his responsibilities to heart. The country could do so much for its' people. Hannes was a father first and a politician second.

Vilborg rushed back to the house and found that Hannes had already left for the office. Vilborg was anxious to speak to Hannes as ideas were bouncing around in her head. She couldn't sit still and just wait for him to return at the end of a very long day. Vilborg set to getting her daily work done at the house and when she was satisfied that she had completed all of her tasks in her usual fastidious manner, she set out to find Hannes Hafstein in his office. She did not have an appointment but expected that she would need to wait until he was free to see her. Hopefully he was in the office and not out and about meeting with his people.

Vilborg arrived at his office in Akureyi and was relieved to find that he was indeed in his office — he was busy working on a speech so he was able to meet with her right away.

Hannes was quite surprised to see Vilborg at his office and exclaimed that something serious must be happening as she had never visited him outside of his home before. Vilborg passionately explained the plan that she had roughly formed with her faery friend Shelley. As expected, Hannes did not dismiss her but listened intently to her plea for help.

After some deep discussion and questions back and forth, Hannes jumped up and exclaimed, "I have been struggling myself with the plight of the Icelandic peoples and have spent many a sleepless night considering what could be done to help so many people. No one is immune to the disasters befalling the country — the sickness does not seem to care whom you are, where you come from, how much tragedy you have already suffered, nor does it distinguish the poor from the wealthy. All of us are at risk!"

Hannes rounded his desk, caught Vilborg in an embrace and declared "I promise to take your plan to parliament and will do all I can to ensure that all the regional representatives of government are in attendance so that we can make this idea of yours a reality. ""I love your idea of meeting at Pingfella — even though we no longer meet there — it would be a strong message of unity and country spirit if we did so as we bring together a plan with the hidden peoples and the Icelandic parliament."

In a short amount of time, Hannes called upon the regional representatives of government and sent out an invitation to Queen Hildur of the Hidden People.

Queen Hildur in turn met with Shelley and ensured that all of the elders of the hidden peoples and faeries of the regional areas of Iceland were summoned to a meeting in a secret location. Many of the elders held deep to their beliefs that modern Icelanders were not receptive to meet any hidden people or faeries and were in fact, quite terrified of them.

Much discussion ensued and Queen Hildur and Shelley were able to sway the elders to consider the development of a plan to encourage participation by the younger faeries and hidden people to engage in deep and lasting friendships with those small Icelandic children who had lost a parent or two to the sickness sweeping through the nation.

After much debate, Queen Hildur stood and softly pronounced, "I have never been more proud or appreciative of my heritage and the kindness of the elders as I am today. You have my sincere thanks for your commitment to this plan. I have every confidence that your friendships will be life altering for so many of us and for the young children of Iceland."

Queen Hildur chose a Pixie as they were faeries that was best suited to working with small children. Pixies were known to be very social and much more active than other forms of faeries. Queen Hildur knew in her heart that the mission would be successful if the right faery for the task was selected.

Hannes Hafstein had equal success with his meeting with the regional representatives of government at their meeting at Pingfella.

Queen Hildur and Hannes Hafstein met again to finalize the details of the joint plan between the Icelandic government and the hidden peoples of Iceland, a plan to bring solace and companionship to all of the small children and shattered families affected by the sickness.

And so, it was proclaimed.

Chapter 1
Iceland — 1912

Young Hjortur was born in 1906 and raised in the north of Iceland on a rugged coastline facing the Artic Ocean to the northwest and the sweep of a mountain to the southeast.

Hjortur's family lived just north along the coast from the family farm of his mother at Mana. Life was full of hardships. Siglufjordur was the small village that served the little farms and access to Siglufjordur was made as one went up and over the mountain range behind Mana down into the valley to Siglufjordur.

Hjortur was a slight lad with gangly arms and legs worn thin with the constant effort of tending to the sheep in difficult terrain. He had a mop of blonde hair that curled in the damp weather and he was forever grateful when it was time to shear the sheep for it was then that he was able to have his own mop of hair sheared to a fine brush cut. He hated his curls and the speed at which it would grow; he felt quite feminine with the unruliness of his hair and how it would get in his way in the wind. Grandmother Johanna saw to it that he always had a knitted cap to wear to tame his hair. The shearing occurred sometime in November, so Hjortur was blessed with a boyish cut during the Christmas season when all relatives seemed to gather at Grandmother Johanna's farm.

A terrible sickness swept through the neighbouring farms in the fall of 1912. The Christmas season of 1912 was particularly difficult as no family came to visit and Hjortur's family was unable to travel. It was awfully quiet at the farm with his mother Johanna and his father. Hjortur's mother fell victim to the sickness. Johanna had become quite ill during the shearing season and took to her bed. Hjortur was aware of her sickness but was not aware of the seriousness of her condition. "Father, when will Mother be better?" Hjortur asked his father. "Will she be better by Christmas so that we can journey down the way to Grandmother Johanna's?"

"Yes, son. Your mother will get better. She is almost over the worst of it now. You go and tend to the sheep. I will keep watch over your mother" his father responded. Hjortur's face lit with pleasure and the anticipation of his mother being well again. He headed out of doors to do his chores and returned to the house as darkness was falling. He was surprised to see the doctor sitting at the kitchen table comforting his father who was sobbing uncontrollably.

"Father, what is it, what is wrong? Is it Mother?" whispered Hjortur. The doctor looked up at Hjortur and motioned for him to follow.

"Hjortur, I am afraid that your mother has died. She was unable to fight this terrible illness. Your father is devastated and I don't believe he will be of any comfort to you. He is not doing well. You also need to be aware that we are placing your farm under quarantine. No one is allowed to enter the farmyard or house, nor are any of you permitted to leave. You will have to make do with what food supplies you have. This illness has no name and we do not know how to stop the spread therefore you cannot be allowed to venture out and possibly spread the illness. You need to be aware as well, that while you are not sick yet, that you may become ill yourself. I have been watching your father closely and so far he is not showing any signs of illness. Unfortunately, he is not strong enough to fight off such an illness if he were to be infected. He is not a man of strong emotional fortitude. Your mother was the strength in your family. It will be up to you now to keep the farm running smoothly and to tend to the animals until your father gets back on his feet." stated the doctor. "Do you understand Hjortur?" asked the doctor. "Do you think you can cope with the demands to be placed on your young shoulders?"

"Yes, I think I can. Father just needs to rest." Hjortur stuttered out his response.

"You are so much your mother's son." responded the Doctor. "You will do well in life. You are a very sensible young man. Be well," said the doctor and took his leave.

The next few weeks passed in a blur. As the farm was under quarantine, it was up to Hjortur and his father to prepare the ground for Johanna and to conduct their own funeral and burial. Because of the illness and the inability of Hjortur to dig a grave, Father assisted Hjortur to wrap Johanna in her bed clothes and blankets and place her in the horse cart. Hjortur had managed to dig a small depression in the ground on which the horse cart was set. Johanna's body was lovingly covered with a blanket and armloads of hay from the barn. Hjortur would have liked to put mountain flowers on the top of the cart but it was December and it was very cold, damp and windy. He did find a special dresser scarf that Johanna had treasured. Hjortur placed the scarf under the hay. Father came out to the burial site and stood with his arms at his sides looking at the cart. Hjortur lit the torch and started the fire to cremate Johanna. Hjortur longed to hold hands with his father but his father was lost in his own world. Both stood perfectly still, remembering Johanna and her spirit. Hjortur began to sing quietly at first, and when his father didn't object, drew strength from within, began to sing with purpose and love. Hjortur sang until his throat grew parched. Tears streamed down his face. Father stood still until the fire burned down to embers and then he turned, looked at Hjortur and nodded and walked away back to the house. Hjortur stayed behind for some time until the cart and Johanna were smouldering ashes. Then Hjortur began the task of placing the soil back across the mound to make a gravesite. Johanna had taught Hjortur to print the alphabet and he had painstakingly carved the letters of Johanna into the wood from an old chair that he had discovered in the barn. He then found some string and fashioned a cross out of the broken chair pieces.

Once the mound was covered with the dirt and moss from the ground, Hjortur placed the cross on the mound and sang a final song. With a shake of his shoulders, he looked out across the farm to the sea, and slowly walked back to the farmhouse.

Hjortur looked around the house forlornly and shook his head sadly. Father was sitting in his chair staring out the window. He had hardly noticed when Hjortur came in and didn't speak. Night began to fall. Hjortur was too exhausted emotionally to even think of finding something to eat for the both of them. He crossed the room and crawled under the covers of his bed. What on earth was to become of the two of them? Hjortur missed his mother.

Christmas passed and the days passed. Father did manage the get himself back out into the fields and into managing the sheep. Hjortur's days got a little easier but there was no companionship with his father. Each of them fell into their own routine, Father in the fields and Hjortur keeping house and making the meals as well as other farm chores.

Hjortur's father was unable to cope with the loss of his beloved wife and began to lose his mind. His eyesight was failing as well.

Hjortur's Grandmother Johanna who lived at Mana took young Hjortur under her wings and did her best to manage his grief at losing his mother. This was difficult for Grandmother Johanna as it was her daughter Johanna that had passed. Grandmother Johanna's husband Johan had died some six years prior to daughter Johanna.

Grandmother Johanna was full of grief and despair. She had lived a very hard life at Mana and was anxious to go with her son Johan who had immigrated to Canada in 1905.

Johan had returned to Iceland in 1912 as he had heard that his father had passed away in 1906 and his mother was struggling to run the family farm at Mana. Life was a constant struggle.

Love also played a role in the return of Johan from

Canada. Johan had fallen in love with Gudrun who just happened to be the young neighbour girl across the creek from Mana at a thriving sheep farm called Dalabae.

While Grandmother Johanna and Uncle Johan were busy discussing Johan's return to Canada, young Hjortur was sinking deeper and deeper into a depressed state. His father was unable to cope with life and Grandmother Johanna was keeping an eye out for Hjortur but that was the extent of her care of him. He suffered in silence.

Chapter 2
Iceland — 1913

Poppy was a young faery pixie of only nineteen and she was assigned to be the guardian faery for seven-year-old Hjortur. Poppy was a tiny sprite of a thing with soft tightly wound blonde curls that encased her head like a swimming cap. She was delicate and perfectly proportioned. She had sparkling green eyes and a fierce temper. She was 5.5 inches tall and had wings.

She wore a long woolen cape to protect her wings. She would only open and flex her wings on an especially warm day with little wind. She often needed to mend her wings. They required great care and wings were quite versatile. The wings provided a protective covering for the Pixie. The pixie would pull the wings close around the body, lower the head, pull up the knees and curl the legs and the pixie would be totally encased in the cocoon of the wings. Pixies would be safe from predators and the elements. While in the cocoon of the wings, time stood still for the pixie and they sunk into a hypnotic state of hibernation. To avoid such a state, the pixie may have elected to keep the neck and head outside of the cocoon and ease one foot out to the outside elements as a reminder that the body was not preparing to hibernate. These simple measures would enable a cozy sleep for the pixie while still being able to be present in the moment in case of being required for duty to the children.

Poppy had a soft spot for little boys and could match energy for the devilish games young boys could play. But young Hjortur was not a very active young boy. He was extremely quiet and withdrawn. He had suffered so and missed his mother and his father terribly.

Poppy was drawn to his melancholy and was determined more than ever to have this boy return to his previous personality of a little imp who loved to play and run with the animals. Poppy was intrigued to find that Hjortur had soft curls just like her! Whenever possible, Hjortur would have his curls cut short but they always grew back so fast that he constantly wore a knitted cap to hide his curls. Poppy could not figure out why he didn't love his curls as much as she loved her curls!

Poppy and young Hjortur began an amazing friendship based on trust and compassion. Poppy was just what Hjortur needed. Poppy provided warmth and understanding but with a firm hand. Before long, Hjortur was beginning to make progress and was slowly starting to interact with Poppy and the animals. But he was still timid and very much anxious about what would happen to him. He was a very sensitive boy.

Uncle Johan had just married Gudrun in June of 1913. In July 1913, they were to be sailing from Akureyi to Glasgow and then on to Canada with Hjortur's grandmother Johanna and Johan's younger brother Kristen.

After much discussion with Hjortur's father, it was decided that Hjortur would go to Canada with the Grandmother Johanna, Uncle Johan and Aunt Gudrun,

Gudrun's brother Einar and Uncle Kristen and make a new life in Saskatchewan. Poppy was anxious but knew that she must go with Hjortur — he needed her and believed in her. Before long, he would be grown and Poppy could return to Iceland.

It tore at young Hjortur to leave his father behind, but he did recognize that the father he once knew and loved was fading away and there was nothing that Hjortur could do that made a difference in how his father reacted to his surroundings. He was drowning in grief for his dead wife and was unable to cope with the needs of a grieving child. After the wedding celebrations of Johan and Gudrun at Dalabae, the emigrants made their journey up along the pass of the mountain and down into Siglufjordur. From Siglufjordur, Gudrun's brother escorted them to Akureyri to see them off and returned to Dalabae with the horses and cart. Grandmother Johanna and the meager belongings rode in the cart and the others rode the small Icelandic ponies along the dirt path to Akureyri. The hiking and horseback riding gladdened Hjortur as he dearly loved the horses. His family was too poor to afford horses but Aunt Gudrun's family did have access to a few of them and they were beautiful creatures. Each night, Hjortur would sleep with the horses, enjoying their company.

Fortunately, it was summertime and the days were long and warm. They made good time along the way and arrived in Akureyri the evening before the scheduled departure. Young Hjortur was exhausted when they finally arrived at the docks and was looking forward to lazy days aboard ship as was promised him by Uncle

Johan.

The ship sailed from Akureyri to Glasgow and then on to Quebec Canada. Hjortur withdrew further and became even quieter with each passing day on the journey. It was a rough time with days and days of sickness as the open seas tossed the ship about.

Passenger quarters were overcrowded with hopeful emigrants trying to remain positive about their futures. The constant rolling of the ship and the ensuing vomiting terrified Hjortur. His dear mother had succumbed to horrific bouts of vomiting that left her limp and despondent. Her dying was a prolonged affair that had taken its toll on the whole family. Hjortur was not able to hold back his own vomiting and was sure that he was about to die like his mother. Poppy did all she could to comfort and soothe Hjortur. She stayed by his side and whispered words of encouragement in his ear and with her feathery touch, rubbed his back and head to relieve his tensions.

The arrival in Quebec was met with gladness by all of the passengers. Hjortur finally quit vomiting but was suffering from exhaustion and malnutrition caused by the sickness.

Hjortur was lethargic and could barely walk off the ship on his own wobbly legs. Poppy was determined to see him well again and cajoled him into a smile and walking the plank to depart the ship. She encouraged him to kiss the ground and bid farewell to the ship that she promised him he would never have to board again! Sea going excursions were just not for Hjortur. He was set to be a landlubber for life!

Chapter 3
Saskatchewan, Canada — 1913 – 1934

After a number of cramped days travelling aboard a cargo train, the Icelanders arrived in Big Quill Lake, Saskatchewan. Johan looked about the landscape with fondness and excitement. He gazed around his family and saw a very worn out-group of people. He was anxious to begin again in this Promised Land. Johan had first immigrated to Canada in 1905 and purchased a tract of land that he farmed for a number of years. Eventually, a letter had arrived for him from his mother in Iceland. His father had passed away, as had several other members of the community and Johanna was feeling the strain of running the family farm without her husband or her eldest son. Johanna's other children had married and moved away to their own places. She was left with just her youngest son Kristen.

Johanna was thrilled to be able to travel to Canada with Johan and other family to begin a new life.

Young Hjortur settled with Johan and Gudrun in Dafoe and Johanna purchased her own farm nearby. With Poppy at his side, Hjortur was very helpful on the farm and was extremely capable of looking after all of the livestock. Hjortur was very good with the sheep and enjoyed being outside in the very different landscape than that of Iceland. The wide-open spaces of Saskatchewan, the proximity to the lake full of fish, the fertile land that produced huge amounts of grain, was a wonder for Hjortur.

While he thrived in the new environment, he was still experiencing times of melancholy and fear that this life would come to an end. His missed his father and worried about him. He was the only child in this family and was growing up way too fast without being able to enjoy playing. Life was hard, but he was thankful. He had a roof over his head, he never went hungry and he lived with family who all worked hard and were never abusive.

Uncle Johan and Aunt Gudrun and Grandmother Johanna were not used to showing affection for others, however, they were steadfast in their devotion to each other and in the need to make a success of the new farm. There was no time to cuddle and laze about encouraging a child as he learned something new. It was indeed a blessing that Hjortur had Poppy. She provided the much-needed encouragement and affection along the way.

She was still very much needed in Hjortur's life.

Within a year of arriving in Big Quill Lake, Gudrun's brother Einar made the decision to return home to Iceland. Life was not any easier than in Iceland. Working the land was hard work and Einar simply preferred fishing in the ocean rather than a lake; and he missed his family in Dalabae. While Einar made plans to return to Iceland, Poppy anguished over an opportunity to return to Iceland nestled amongst Einar's belongings, but was torn at the thought of leaving Hjortur. It was her assignment to support and befriend Hjortur and he was just not ready for Poppy to leave. Einar returned to

Iceland in early 1914 and Poppy remained in Saskatchewan to care for Hjortur. Unbeknownst to her, another opportunity to return to Iceland would not be forthcoming for another one-hundred years!

Poppy fashioned a tent for her own personal space out of a man's handkerchief. She found pieces of twigs perfectly rounded and weathered by the elements and made a long rafter along the top and held out to the four corners by small pegs broken off of twigs. In the tent, Poppy was able to stand in the center and walk along under the length of the rafter. On one of the two slanted sides, she placed fronds from ferns or nettles from trees for her bed and along the other side, she fashioned a small area to keep her treasures that she collected.

Pillows were fashioned out of the cotton fluff from poplar trees. She sewed them into pieces of a handkerchief and had a lovely soft cushion to lie upon. Cotton fluff was also sewed into a long pouch made from sewing two pieces of handkerchief together and stuffing with cotton fluff to make a cozy down comforter. A second handkerchief was cut to make flaps for each triangle end of the tent so that she could tie back the flaps to allow for air to pass through and for the sunshine to pour in. It was really a lovely small home that she treasured.

Poppy's supply of men's handkerchiefs never ended as the handkerchief was a staple for all of the men. With their Nordic genes, the noses of the men were substantial in size and required a large sized handkerchief to properly tend to the needs of the nose. Laundering of the handkerchiefs was constant and hanging of the laundry ensured constant bleaching by the sun.

When Johan came back to Canada, he changed the family name to Dalman from Bjornson as it was confusing to non-Icelanders to grasp the different last names within a household for the male and female members. Hjortur felt at odds with the name change and was again discontent for a period of time. Poppy noticed his withdrawal and was determined to have a conversation with Hjortur. Hjortur had become very intent on working hard to assist the Dalman family but Poppy did manage to sit Hjortur down for a much-needed chat.

Hjortur was torn about the name change as he was very grateful to all of the Dalman's, especially Johan who had made a home for Hjortur. But Hjortur felt the ties of loyalty and pride of his own father. He wanted to retain his own family name of Jacobson. Poppy was delighted to get to the bottom of Hjortur's dilemma and encouraged Hjortur to talk to Johan.

As always, Poppy insisted that Hjortur make his own decisions based on faith, honesty, gratitude and kindness. Johan was very much a man's man and was impressed with the loyalty that Hjortur felt for his father back in Iceland. Johan expressed to Hjortur that he too had struggled with the name change to Dalman and whether or not to include Hjortur as a Dalman. Family ties were strong and Hjortur and Johan were able to move ahead in their relationship from one of protector to one of mutual respect, friendship and a deep and abiding love of their Icelandic heritage. Johan was very much impressed with the man that young Hjortur had become. Hjortur was blessed. Poppy beamed with pride.

In short order, Johan and Gudrun had four children and it was a good thing that Hjortur was around to help. This family life assisted greatly in Hjortur overcoming his grief and he began to settle in nicely with life in Canada. The first of the children, a boy named Olafur was born in 1914, followed by Sigrun in 1915, Erla in 1916 and Margret in 1919.

While Johan did elect to change the family name to Dalman, he held strong to his Icelandic heritage and insisted that his four eldest children and Hjortur learned his mother tongue.

He hired a fellow to come to the house to teach the five children to read and write Icelandic, so they all knew how to do so before they ever started school.

Bad luck followed the Dalman family for many years, and that meant several moves from different communities and farms. Weather played a large role as did the depression years of the thirties. Hjortur moved along with the family and attended school here and there.

Hjortur had a very strong work ethic and began working for farmers in his early teens. Hjortur was a saver and was very grateful for the home that the Dalman's provided him. He shared his wealth but was keen to save his money to buy a grain truck. His truck was the first good truck in the area and he hauled grain for many years. He didn't just haul grain. The kind man that he was, Hjortur would transport others to and from activities around the communities.

Chapter 4
Saskatchewan, Canada — 1934 – 1942

Hjortur, with the guidance of Poppy, became a strong influence on the children of Johan and Gudrun. Gudrun was ill for many years and had not been able to raise their third daughter, Margret, born in 1919. Margret was raised by neighbourhood friends from a very early age and it always had seemed the wrong time to bring her home to the Dalman's on the few occasions when Gudrun was feeling somewhat well. And so, Margret stayed with the neighbours and was eventually adopted by them. From 1914 to 1932 Johan and Gudrun had ten children. Around this time, Hjortur had developed a relationship with the neighbor girl. As the year progressed Hjortur proposed marriage to her. Poppy was ecstatic at the marriage of Hjortur and his sweetheart and was busy herself at that time as Johan and Gudrun had just had their tenth child Svienne. It was time for Poppy to transition her assignment from Hjortur to Svienne.

Poppy had been just begun caring for Svienne when he was two and fell down into a smoldering fire pit and badly burned his right hand, losing part of his pinky finger. Svienne experienced considerable pain and had to relearn how to use his hand as the fingers had webbed together with the severity of the burn. Poppy would massage Svienne's hand to soothe his pain. To quieten

Svienne, Poppy would play tickling games with him by driving his toy cars along his body to help him relax and sleep. This method of relaxation stayed with Svienne for many years as he encouraged his own children to drive toy cars on his back, head and neck. For many years Svienne coped with a webbed hand. He did regain use of the hand but required constant nursing to assist the hand and to be free from infection.

Sister Erla did help him as Gudrun was very ill at the time. But Erla was a busy woman of nineteen, running the household for Gudrun and was not able to provide the comfort that dear Svienne required. As a result, Poppy found herself spending more and more time with Svienne and a deep love and friendship formed. Svienne needed Poppy and believed in her. Poppy nurtured Svienne and encouraged him to be a child. He was extremely sensitive and a very lonely boy. Svienne was especially slight and fair headed. He too, had a head full of curls!

Born during the depression, Svienne was often left alone while other members of the household worked hard to keep food on the table. It was a very hard life. There was a time before his mother passed that Poppy would find him laughing and running about the farmyard as he chased the animals about. He was a mischievous child and delighted his mother with his teasing manner. As he was unable to manage many of the farm tasks, he often spent time indoors chatting softly and making his mother comfortable. Poppy was amazed at the depth of compassion that such a young boy could muster realizing that he was coping with a dying mother.

But Svienne did not understand that Gudrun was

failing. He always hoped that he could coax her into rising from her bed to look out and see the beauty of the land or watch the animals from her window. On the day prior to her death, Svienne had been unable to get Gudrun to raise her head off of her pillow so he brought in a small kitten to snuggle with her. He was so pleased with himself. Gudrun's face lit up and she beamed with pleasure.

Gudrun died at the age of forty-four leaving seven-year-old Svienne without a mother. Svienne was completely devastated at her death and withdrew further into himself. He missed her so. He spent much of his time cuddling and cooing to the kitten, but he rarely spoke out loud. Poppy was afraid that Svienne would forget how to speak. The only sounds to come from him were the sounds he would make when speaking to the animals. She would have been very worried if Svienne did not speak to her. But he did in his own very soft manner.

When Poppy got him talking, she couldn't stop the floodgates that opened as Svienne reminisced about his mother and her last days. No one else in the household had any time for Svienne. They were all having a difficult time and dealing with a young child was not something that any of them considered to be of importance. It was still the depression, there was a world war happening and the younger children of the family had to learn to cope with hardships.

Johan was blindsided by Gudrun's death. While it was true that she had been ill for very many years, he did not expect that she would die at such a young age. He was filled by grief and was unable to offer solace to any of his children. He kept to himself and busied himself with work.

Svienne turned to Poppy and together they spent time with the animals in the fields. Svienne yearned for a family and a sense of belonging. Poppy encouraged Svienne with his drawings. Svienne would often be found alone with his thoughts and his pencil and would be drawing or carving pieces of wood into magical works of art. He had such a talent. Svienne became quite adept at using a pencil with his webbed hand. Svienne also loved to hum. He connected to the animals with his quiet manner and soft humming as he puttered about the farmyard.

In the Fall of 1939, Erla moved to Victoria to live with their brothers Runar and Snorri.

The other siblings stayed behind in Saskatchewan. It wasn't long before Runar, Snorri and Erla had married. Svienne had been sent to live with his older brother Olafur and his wife Dagny. Eleven-year-old Ragnar was sent to live with sister Sigrun and her husband Isak.

Seven-year-old Svienne struggled with the arrangement with Olafur and Dagny. Olafur was newly married at twenty-five and was not particularly interested in raising his youngest brother who was so young and was deformed at that. Svienne tried his very best to assist on the farm, but he did not have the strength for full use of his right hand. With the extra mouth to feed, Olafur had expectations that Svienne could perform some of the farm chores. He was bitterly disappointed in Svienne and was unable to hide his disdain. Svienne struggled with any of the chores assigned to him and dearly wanted to be left alone so that he could attend school.

Chapter 5
Victoria, Vancouver Island, Canada —
1943 – 1960

In 1943, Svienne was eleven years old. He was still struggling with the use of his webbed right hand. It was evident that Svienne was not happy with Olafur and Dagny, and it was suggested that farming was not to be an option for Svienne so he was sent off to Victoria to live. Poppy went along to care for Svienne who was still broken hearted at the loss of his mother. Svienne was sent to live with his sister Erla and her husband Sindri.

Poppy had journeyed from Iceland, to Glasgow, to Saskatchewan and now to Victoria on Vancouver Island. Poppy was thrilled to live again near the coast. It seemed that a return to Iceland was not possible at this time. Poppy dearly missed her family and friends back in Iceland.

While Erla and her husband Sindri spoke Icelandic at home, young Svienne did not. The language barrier continued to deepen the rift that prevented any closeness developing between the siblings. Poppy often reminisced about Iceland when Erla and Sindri were speaking in their hushed voices to avoid being noticed by Svienne. It was a difficult time for them all. Erla was trying to be the perfect wife while raising a sulky, depressed young brother.

Soon after the arrival of Svienne, Erla was pregnant with their first child and was quite sickly with the pregnancy. Svienne was left to do her bidding and was run off his feet trying to keep the house tidy and presentable when Sindri returned at the end of a long day.

Erla was only agreeable when Svienne managed to have the house ship shape. He also began to cook and bake so that Erla could gain strength as her pregnancy progressed.

Svienne was resentful. There were little thanks for his diligence and hard work. He was still a boy and worked very hard to be part of a family. He was lonely. He did attend school and excelled at sports. Any musical inclination he had was squashed for lack of time and money. When the new baby girl Katla was born, Svienne had hoped that life would return to some sort of normal and he could spend some time with the neighbourhood children playing outside. But it was not to be.

Sindri was not happy about being forced to feed another mouth at his table. He believed that Svienne had to earn his keep, regardless of his age. By now, Svienne was thirteen years old, and he spent every day after school assisting Erla around the house with the chores, dishes and playing with young Katla. On weekends, Svienne attended work with Sindri as a gopher running back and forth with supplies trying to anticipate what Sindri might need next.

Another baby was to be born and Svienne again assumed many of the household duties. Poppy kept a close watch on Svienne encouraging him to be thankful for being raised in such a beautiful city away from the farmlands. He lived in a new house surrounded by family. But it was not Svienne's family, and he still felt the animosity that oozed from Sindri. Erla tried to squash the tension in the household, but Sindri did not want Svienne living with them, nor acting the big brother to his daughter and newly born son. So, the pair kept Svienne busy so they could raise their children.

Poppy constantly mentored Svienne into seeing the positive side of his circumstances and encouraging him to believe in a family of his own one day. To have his own family, Svienne would need a proper job, a career. His siblings had varied careers. Some were electricians. Others were farmers and fishermen. With the onset of the war, his older brothers had joined the army. Sadly, his nineteen-year-old brother Bjarni had died in Holland. He never had a chance to live or to have a family. This tragedy did enable Svienne to push through his own depression and to plan for the future.

Sindri realized that Svienne had potential to be a good electrician, but the webbed right hand was posing a problem with dexterity. Erla researched the possibility of surgery and spoke with her sister-in-law who worked in a doctor's office. It wasn't long before an opportunity for surgery arose.

Svienne was scheduled for skin to be grafted from his chest to his hand to cut away the webbing that resulted from the fall into the fire. The surgery was a huge success but very painful. Svienne was thrilled with his right hand and vowed to never complain again of any need to do chores. He healed fast and was very energetic in his desire to help out Sindri at work. And Sindri was right. With the improved use of his hand, Svienne was as natural as an electrician. His work was always neat and tidy. Svienne took great pride in his abilities and in how his perfectionism in running wires caused others to stare in amazement at the tidiness. Svienne was quick and he was particular. And other electricians wanted Svienne to work for them.

He made it his mission to be eager to help Johann with his work as an electrician and learn all he could. He excelled at lacrosse at school. He excelled in the arts. And he remembered how to hum again.

Now that Svienne had showed his potential in the working world, Sindri did not share Svienne with Erla to assist with the household chores. Sindri made good use of Svienne's talents and pushed him to the limits. Svienne was encouraged to quit school to work full time with Sindri. This bothered Poppy but she kept silent as Svienne was finally letting go of some of his anger at life and getting on with finding himself. Quitting school meant giving up on high school lacrosse and that was a tough blow for Svienne. He was proud of his talent on the courts and his friends were sad to see him go. They came from solid middle-class families and were able to stay at school and graduate. This departure from school would torture Svienne in his future years.

Svienne met Ellie at a friend's house at a party. Ellie was a very beautiful young woman and had already quit school to go to work. She was a hard worker and so fun. Svienne fell for her love of life and her laughter. They made a handsome couple. Svienne was just nineteen, and

Ellie seventeen, when they married. Svienne was so pleased that he had a wife and a career as an electrician. He was blessed. Poppy helped to instill in Svienne a very strong work ethic, appreciation of his surroundings, respect and honesty. Svienne was a sensitive man and was easily insulted. Often times, Ellie had to watch her tongue to ensure that she had not unwittingly said something that was taken in the wrong way.

One year after their marriage, a son was born. Tux was a very big baby but such a happy fellow. As seemed to be the norm for the Icelandic men, Tux also had a mass of curls!

Svienne was over-the-moon in love with his child and was determined that he would never ever feel the emptiness that Svienne felt during his childhood. He was bitter about being raised by his sister and her husband. Svienne was proud of his relationship with his in-laws and learned a tremendous amount from his father-in-law about finances and building. Svienne and Ellie lived in several homes before they were able to build a home of their very own.

By the time they were able to move into their newly built home, a daughter Isabelle was born. Life was so perfect. He had a wife, a son and a daughter of his own. Oddly, Isabelle was quite bald at birth but by the age of two eventually grew bits of hair to cover the veins on her head. Poppy found it very weird that the boys had curly hair and this baby girl had no hair! Svienne continued to work hard to feed and clothe his family. Having his own close-knit family was very important to him. Svienne continued to struggle emotionally about his childhood and Poppy would surface and work with him to resolve his imbalance. When he got back on track and was feeling content again, Poppy would relax and settle into her very quiet life. It was at these times that Poppy would seek refuge in her wings and hibernate for months at a time.

His father Johan came to live with him when his wife Ellie was pregnant with their third child. Johan got to know his grandson, Tux, and granddaughter, Isabelle.

Chapter 6
Victoria and Nanaimo, Vancouver Island, Canada — 1960 – 1977

In Grandfather Johan's mind, girls were not afforded the time and affection that a boy child warranted. Johan enjoyed playing games with the grandchildren but was blatant in his preference for his grandson. While playing store with the grandchildren, Johan would provide real money to his grandson and play money to his granddaughter. Johan considered the hurt of his granddaughter to be insolence. The grandchildren enjoyed spending time with Johan and loved the sailboat that he would craft out of a tobacco pouch. However, Isabelle felt shunted by her grandfather and was shocked to meet Poppy one day. Isabelle believed in faeries and was enthralled with Poppy and a deep friendship evolved.

Isabelle and Tux had a close relationship and spent much time playing around their neighbourhood. Next door to their home, a small-forested area bordered a farmyard. Many hours were spent climbing trees and exploring while Poppy kept watch.

To reach the school grounds, the children would venture across the street along a dirt path to a field bordering the school grounds. Over the school year, a path was worn across the field. One day, several girl friends of Isabelle were upset at a group of boys who had gathered garter snakes and viciously sliced them up and sprinkled them along the worn path so that the girls could not get to school. It was unthinkable that the girls would be late for school, which they would be if they had to make their way back along the street and around the block to the school. Isabelle, with Poppy sitting on her shoulder, braved the horror, and kicked all of the snake parts off of the path into the tall grass so that her friends could run along the path to school. Isabelle was the hero of the day, and the boys were grudgingly respectful of Isabelle for many years after.

A favourite hangout for the children was Sherwood Forest that was on the far side of the schoolyard and down the street some distance. The entrance to Sherwood Forest was across from that street and was quite shaded and spooky. This was not a place that Isabelle and Tux went on their own but rather when a group of children got together to explore, Sherwood Forest was a great place. Safety in numbers! Robin Hood was the favorite game to play and Poppy helped out with bravery. Isabelle thought of the dangers of ticks but once engulfed in the magic of Sherwood Forest, such fears were forgotten and make believe diverted all other thoughts.

Often times, Isabelle would be in charge of her sisters and would leave the house early in the day for an adventure. Tiny LeeBones, with her mass of blonde curls, would be placed in the bicycle basket up front and Annie Oakley, with the thick, straight dark hair, would sit on the bicycle seat and hang on for dear life as Isabelle stood and pedaled her way along the roads to visit other children. Poppy did wonder at the differences in the children's hair. Poppy certainly loved her own blonde, springy curls. Isabelle's body would be sashaying back and forth with the up and down of the pedaling as she struggled to maintain control over the bicycle and to see over Little LeeBones. It would be catastrophic to hit a hole in the road. There were a few instances that one or both of the little sisters were dumped off the bicycle but it was never on the pavement. When Isabelle did lose control of the bicycle, it was because she was riding fast over the beaten path and the little sisters were flung into the tall grass. But the girls did not speak of those times as the little sisters loved to go out and about with their big sister. Poppy kept a close eye out for any injuries.

There was a time that Isabelle got sidetracked by the pleasures of play and left her little sisters with the mum of a child that she was playing with. It was a good thing that Poppy had hopped off and kept with the little sisters. Isabelle did remember her little sisters after a few hours and went back to gather them up and head home.

It was Poppy who was the voice of reason and encouraged Isabelle to be mature and responsible. Tux was often in awe of Isabelle who was younger than he, but Tux did not meet Poppy nor was he aware that Poppy was the influence over Isabelle that gave Isabelle the aura of calm and responsibility.

Isabelle possessed a natural shyness that she strove to overcome. Poppy worked tirelessly with Isabelle to aid her in her efforts. Isabelle developed several close friendships with some classmates in junior high school. The three became bosom buddies and it was Isabelle that the group turned to for relationship advice. The trio spent many hours pondering future lives and situations. Again, Isabelle was blessed with the support and mentoring of Poppy who guided Isabelle through the many trials of a very shy teenager.

As she had set the standard with her previous charges, Poppy instilled the basic premise of hard work, honesty and integrity within Isabelle. With these codes of conduct at her side, Isabelle developed close friendships that stood the test of time. Respect and diversity were the foundations of the friendships and guided the girls on their journey through life and relationships.

After many years, Isabelle married her sweetheart, George. They had a lovely family of three children — Turkey, Beannie and Froggie.

Chapter 7
Victoria, Vancouver Island, and Northern British Columbia, Canada

1985 – 2009

Isabelle had a daughter, Beannie, who was an avid reader and wanted more than anything to go to school like her dad. Beannie met Poppy when she was just three. Poppy recognized that Beannie was an explorer and a true believer of faeries. Beannie did lack confidence and looked to Poppy to give her the push to follow through with her curiosity and desire to learn.

When Beannie was four, the family moved from Vancouver Island away from the coast to Northern British Columbia to the mountains. This was a huge shock for Poppy for she had gotten very used to the mild climate and weekly visits to the seashores along the coast.

The smell and sounds of the ocean had invaded her senses and reminded her of her home in Iceland. Contrary to popular belief, the north of Iceland was really quite similar in temperature to that of the southern coast of British Columbia. Almost seventy-five years had passed since Poppy had left her homeland and she still suffered bouts of homesickness. When these bouts became unbearable, she simply cocooned herself into her wings, tucked in her neck and head, pulled up her knees and feet and slept deeply. When her self-imposed hibernation was complete, she would awake refreshed and ready to take on her responsibilities looking out for the welfare of whichever child she was currently mentoring. It was a fairly lonely life as she was very capable in her teachings and all of her charges had become capable, happy adults and she would find herself with too much time on her hands and pondering about life of her family and friends back in Iceland.

Poppy found Northern British Columbia to be absolutely stunning with the majestic mountains and waterways. She soon settled into the life of Isabelle's family and contented herself with keeping Beannie in line.

Beannie was bossy and bold when she was confident. Beannie was the middle child with a much older brother and a little baby brother. As Beannie got braver, she often engaged her brothers in her plans to change things. Her older brother, Turkey, would attempt to cajole her into being a tomboy but she shied away from his attempts to toughen her up.

She had her own ideas of what she wanted to do and would turn the tables on Turkey. Her baby brother, Froggie, was often the brunt of her experiments with her ideas. She would set him up and send him on his way, and if he were successful, she would push on and move ahead in her pursuit of her latest idea. If he were unsuccessful in his mission, she would simply abandon her baby brother and run away in defeat. Over time, her younger brother caught on and turned the tables on her practices. Turkey and Froggie soon learned that they had to outsmart Beannie.

Each of Isabelle and George's children were musical and all of them had lessons. Turkey chose the piano and guitar and did perform a lovely duet with George when he was just five years old. *"Old Lord It's Hard to Be Humble"* was a big hit with the small community performance. Turkey loved the admiration but choose to discontinue his studies in music by the time he was ten. It was too much of a chore for him. Froggie took piano lessons and did perform in a recital at the age of five but was not impressed at all by the requirements for practice. He did not continue his studies.

Beannie was an incredible musician with a haunting voice and a passion for learning a musical instrument. Poppy would sit on her shoulder and peer down at the instrument and be in awe at the sounds that Beannie could create. With Poppy nearby, Beannie gained more and more confidence and blossomed into a fine musician and singer. Beannie found the courage to sing for small audiences and even managed to brave singing and playing the guitar for an auditorium full of her peers at an assembly. Beannie was gaining momentum with her musical talents and was asked to play guitar at her graduation ceremonies. She did so with great aplomb and was given a standing ovation for her performance.

The area that Isabelle's family moved to in Northern British Columbia was to one of heavy snowfall. Many years previous to their coastal living, Isabelle and George had invested in snow machines. Being the older child, Turkey had loads of experience on the snow machines and was able to share his knowledge about the operation of the snow machines with his siblings. Neither Beannie nor Froggie were big enough to drive the machines on their own, but they loved to sit behind Turkey as he maneuvered the machine. These machines had been in storage and were now in use with the abundance of snow.

While Poppy had her wings to provide her with protection from the elements, they did not provide her with ample warmth to allow her to experience the snow. Beannie, with the assistance of her little brother Froggie, created inside pockets on their snowsuits that Poppy could ride in. And ride, she did! How exhilarating!

It was a law that George had insisted upon that everyone riding on a snow machine must wear a helmet! Beannie and Froggie came up with a plan to create a helmet out of a walnut shell. The half shell fit perfectly but they struggled with something to hold the helmet in place and to protect Poppy's eyes. Small elastic bands suited for tiny braids were used along with a pair of plastic eyeglasses that Beannie had found for her Barbie doll. Perfect fit! Beannie also found a pair of high plastic fashion boots that Barbie had and bound Poppy's feet with toilet paper squares to ensure a snug fit. Poppy's hands were tucked into a crocheted neck scarf that the Turkey had made for Poppy that Barbie could also use. Poppy was toasty warm! The inside pocket of the snowsuit had been sewn towards the top of the front near the zipper so that Poppy could nestle inside and be able to stand up and peer up and out whenever she felt the zipper being pulled down a bit. When that happened, she knew that it was safe to get up for the snow machine had stopped. The noise of the snow machine terrified Poppy but it was blissfully quiet and so very beautiful when they stopped. The children were happy to be out of doors and riding the snow machines. As the children grew older and bigger, Turkey had moved away and now Froggie was the faster driver and Beannie was much more cautious.

Poppy grew to love the north and the times that they played on the snow machines. It was a great family time. A huge roaring fire was always built, and a picnic outdoors was a lavish spread. Poppy found it quite difficult to try and bite into a piece of wiener, but it was incredibly delicious. If she couldn't manage to finish it, the dog always helped her out.

The most fascinating part of the picnic was the large round squishy white things. The children put them on a stick and stuck them in the fire and they grew larger and turned a lovely golden colour, for those patient enough, to go slow. Other times, the white ball caught on fire and became a black glob! Poppy did try and bite into the things. They were called marshmallows and were very sweet and delicious! The children ate several of them and also shared with the dog that loved to hide them in the snow! Such crazy fun!

After living in a house in town for a number of years, the family fell in love with a property at the base of a ski hill in the mountains. All of the family, including Ellie, were involved in the building of a new family home. Skiing had not been a passion, but it soon became a favorite sport along with the snowmobiling.

The sight of the equipment for the skiing unblocked memories for Poppy as she recalled her early days in Saskatchewan watching Grandmother Johanna cross country skiing.

On one particularly warm winter day in Saskatchewan, the neighbourhood was preparing to have a cross-country ski race and old Grandmother Johanna who was seventy-two years old at the time invited herself to be included in the race. The participants were incredulous but allowed her to race believing her to be a crazy old woman who just might hurt herself. On your mark, get set, go! And Grandmother Johanna was off and without poles she skied across the course and back again before the others had barely made a start! She finished in record time and was first! The rest of the participants were astounded, and Grandmother Johanna was so very pleased with herself! The family rooted and cheered and from there on there was much respect for Grandmother Johanna and her skiing abilities.

Poppy was happy and sad at the same time with the memories that the ski equipment had evoked. She had been in Canada since 1913 and it was now eighty-one years since she had been home. And Poppy was tired. Her cocooning was becoming more and more frequent and she wondered if there would ever be a time when she could return home to Iceland.

Poppy spoke to Beannie about her memories and how long she had been in Canada. Beannie had no idea that Poppy was so old! Each time that Poppy rested in her cocoon, time seemed to stand still and she had not aged much at all. She was still as energetic as she had been as a girl of nineteen but she was much slower.

Beannie chatted to Froggie and he determined that Poppy should have a real home of her own. Isabelle drove

Froggie to the rock quarry in the mountains and he selected some wonderfully coloured slate for the house and roof. Back at the house, he used his father's tools to build a house for Poppy. He found leftover cement powder that his father had used and mixed it up to apply to the slate. Before long, a sturdy slate house had been erected. A base was built and filled with dirt and placed on top of a tree stump. The house was very heavy and it took both Beannie and Froggie all of their strength to set the house up on top of the dirt on the tree stump. They planted flowers around the house and stood back in admiration.

Poppy was summoned and she cried in amazement at the wonderful little slate house.

While Poppy would not be returning to Iceland in the near future, she now had a home of her own. She was blessed and she could feel the love that her adopted family had for her.

Chapter 8
Northern British Columbia, Canada —
2009 – 2017

Over the years, Beannie and Froggie also grew up and moved away from home. Poppy spent more and more time cocooned in her wings, all the while enjoying her lovely slate home. But she was not needed and that saddened her greatly. Isabelle and George worked extended hours and drove great distances to and from work. Work situations changed and Isabelle and George found themselves living in another community for work and returning to the mountain home on weekends. Poppy was so very tired and still homesick. It felt as if Poppy had been retired and was no longer needed. Poppy dreamed of going home to Iceland.

Isabelle and George were blessed with eight grandchildren and spent as much time with them as they possibly could. The one grandson did spend time in the mountains as a young child, but it was the granddaughters who were regular visitors to the mountain home. Make believe became the norm whenever the younger granddaughters came to visit and as part of the make believe, each of the granddaughters were nicknamed after a queen based on their middle names. Queen Marie of Romania, Queen Elizabeth of the United Kingdom,

Queen Ruth of Botswana, Pirate Queen Grace of Ireland, and Queen Isabella of Spain. One granddaughter was older and was not part of the make believe and another granddaughter lived far away and did not travel to the mountain home to visit.

It was so delightful to have young children in the mountain home again. Most weekends would find Isabelle and George returning to the mountain and with them the arrival of the granddaughters. Skiing had become a great passion for the family and once the babies became older, George had them out on the slopes learning to ski.

With so many granddaughters, tea parties became a hit at the mountain home. When they were quite small, Isabelle and George had found a delightful demitasse set of teacups just the perfect size for the little ones to hold and drink from. As they grew up, on their tenth birthdays, a special teacup with their birth month flower was searched out and purchased for the granddaughters. This became a rite of passage of sorts as the girls graduated from the demitasse cups to the larger teacups of their very own. The teacups were so pretty on the table. Gracie had the snowdrops, Lizzie had the roses, Ruth had the holly, Isabelle had the marigolds and Marie had the cosmos. Each one was as unique and beautiful as the granddaughters.

When Isabelle was a young girl, she had visited her Aunt Erla and had been introduced to "mollies"." These "mollies" were actually sugar cubes! Isabelle had never before seen one and was amazed at them. Her aunt showed her that you could dip the sugar cube in your tea and suck the tea right out of them! They were yummy! But children were limited to two mollies. One molly was for the tea and was for dipping! In later years, Isabelle remembered being in a lineup at school eating a molly laced with the polio vaccine. These were much better than getting a needle for a vaccine!

Isabelle introduced this practice to her granddaughters and the mollies became a hit with them too! Special silver tongs were used to extract the mollies from the sugar bowl and each girl would place two mollies on her saucer. Isabelle delighted in watching the faces of the granddaughters as they plunked one molly in their teacup and dipped and sucked the tea out of the other one!

On a bright sunny day in February, five-year-old Lizzie was riding up the chairlift with Isabelle. Lizzie was a talker who was plotting and planning out her grand ideas. She never seemed to keep her thoughts to herself and would talk incessantly to whoever would listen to her. In this instance, it was Grandmother Isabelle that Lizzie had as a confidant.

Isabelle was lost in her own thoughts and had to shake herself to make sense of Lizzie's babbling. "My goodness!" thought Isabelle. Lizzie repeated herself. "Grandma, do you believe in faeries?" Isabelle had a flashback and grinned.

"Oh, I most certainly do Lizzie!" she responded. "In fact, I had a faery friend when I was your age. Her name was Poppy!" Isabelle reminisced with Lizzie and began to tell Lizzie all about Poppy.

Isabelle and Lizzie continued to ski for the rest of the

morning and once they had returned to the house for lunch, Isabelle sought out Poppy. Guilt was evident on Isabelle's face as she discovered Poppy cocooned in her wings tucked away on a shelf in the clothes closet. Given the incredible snowpack that accumulated during the winter months at the house, it was simply not possible for Poppy to live in her slate home. The slate home was a summer home in the mountains. Poppy spent the winter months mostly cocooned in her wings now that she had no children to mentor.

Isabelle gathered up a sleepy Poppy and took her to meet Lizzie. It was love at first sight for both of them. Lizzie was a dear little girl, full of excitement and giggles. She was a tiny thing, with huge brown eyes, long thick eyelashes and long brown hair that she was forever brushing off of her face with her hands. Lizzie squealed in delight at Poppy! She began to babble, and Poppy looked up at Isabelle in amazement with a questioning look. Isabelle laughed! In her excitement Lizzie had begun to express herself in French rather than English. Lizzie was in an all-French class at school and was excited to share her new language with anyone that would listen.

Poppy and Lizzie became inseparable. Poppy continued to live at the mountain house and Lizzie returned to her own home during the week and waited anxiously for the weekends when she could return to the mountain.

While Poppy had been snowmobiling with Turkey, Beannie and Froggie, she had never been on a chairlift.

Lizzie created a small sac for Poppy to ride in and

Lizzie tied the sac around her neck and slipped into the top of her jacket. The sac itself worked like a sling as Poppy nestled herself into the sac. When the timing was just right and the day was perfect, Poppy would stand up in the sac, place her bottom on the top side opening of the sac, hold on to either side by the ropes, and sit with her feet dangling down into the sac. What a grand view!

The beauty of the bright blue sky, the glistening white of the snow, and the green swaying branches of the trees all viewed from her perch on Lizzie's shoulder while riding up the mountain on a chair lift! Exquisite! Poppy felt alive again. Lizzie was thrilled with her new faery friend. She had someone to talk to, to share her ideas with and share the wonders of the mountain. And when Lizzie began her descent on skis, Poppy was breathless! Lizzie was so fast and precise. She squealed in delight and hooted and hollered along with Grandma Isabelle just thrilled to be out on the mountain, flying down the hill on skis and experiencing the beauty of the day! Little bits of the sparkles of the snow landed on Poppy's face and she laughed at the cold. Life was grand. The tables had turned, and while Poppy was thinking that it was she who should have been mentoring and guiding Lizzie, it was Lizzie who had given Poppy the gift of friendship and an appreciation of life. Poppy was blessed with her adopted family. This family nurtured their relationships and each other. Poppy learned again the importance of relationships, respect and gratitude.

PART 2

Chapter 9
Northern British Columbia, Canada —
2009 – 2016

Isabelle and George determined that it was time to retire while they were still young enough to travel. Travelling was a great passion for them and while they had been to a number of exotic locations, several places had yet to be visited.

Froggie became quite interested in researching the family history and found himself stuck when he got to the Dalman/Bjornson side of the family. The Icelandic language made it difficult to research the history, so he pleaded to Isabelle to help him out with the many blank spots in his history.

Family history had always been an area of interest for Isabelle but she never found the time to research while she was working. However, once she was retired, she had some time to dig into stories and her memories of her family.

Before long, Isabelle had cleaned up and made a number of additions to the growing history that Froggie had started. Tux shared a book of Icelandic emigrants in the Saskatchewan area that he had bought for Svienne and Ellie. Isabelle spent some time reading through the book focusing on the stories relevant to Johan and

Hjortur. Isabelle was delighted to find information regarding the location of the marriage of Johan and Gudrun in Iceland. They were married in Dalabae, Iceland in 1913. Much research by Isabelle ensued and it was determined that while Dalabae did not exist in 2016, the name could be broken down to determine the origin. It was also a mystery as to how Johan had come by the name of Dalman to replace the name of Bjornson that he came to Canada as. Both Dalman and Dalabae began with Dal or Dale, which means a wide valley. Dalman could mean man of the valley. Bae was used in the 1500's to refer to sheep sounds.

Isabelle did find a small town called Dalvik just north of Akureyri in northern Iceland. In ancient Nordic history, Vik meant Bay. So, if the town referred to a wide valley near a bay, then it was possible that Dalvik was the Dalabae (wide valley near a bay?) referred to in the historical reference in the book Tux had shared with Isabelle. Perhaps Dalvik was the town her grandparents were married in.

It became very important to Isabelle and George to travel to Iceland to see where her grandparents had immigrated from and to see if they could find the location where her grandparents were married. Language would surely be a barrier, but Isabelle did have the name references to go by and the dates of the marriage and the voyage to Canada were proven to be factual and were tracked on the Ancestry website. Isabelle and George did not have much else to rely on as they began to plan their trip to Iceland.

Isabelle did spend some time trying to chat with

Poppy to determine if she could recall any details, but Poppy was simply confused at the questioning by Isabelle. Isabelle let it drop and did not go into much detail about the trip to Iceland as it was sure to upset Poppy.

Isabelle and George had little faith that they would succeed in finding the location of the marriage of Johan and Gudrun, but it would be rather challenging to give it a try. Both of them were up for the challenge!

Plans were made and Isabelle and George set off on their journey to Iceland. After exploring for several days in and around Reykjavik, they headed northeast into central Iceland with their rental car. The terrain was magnificent and yet harsh. Homes were scattered and little if any landscaping was evident. As they entered into the northern area along the highway where the deep fjords reached down to the land, Isabelle spotted a number of faery houses alongside the road. In recent times, the Icelandic peoples had been known to divert planned roads and excavations if they were told of or were aware of sites of hidden peoples. While no one really admitted to belief of faeries or the hidden people, the Icelanders were not one to challenge the point and simply avoided the areas altogether. Some families were very aware of specific sites of these historic dwellings, and have cordoned off the area with fencing and hedges to assist those who might want to see first-hand where the sites are, and what they look like. To some, this is strictly a ploy to entice tourists to stop and visit, and for others, this is a matter of respect for the faeries and hidden peoples.

Once they had checked into their hotel in Akureyi, Isabelle and George set off to explore the area. They headed out of town and then north to Dalvik. The town was awe-inspiring. It was a fairly small town located at the end of a wide valley and sprawled out along the bay of the fjord. To the left of the town up on the hillside was a small ski hill. Isabelle laughed in delight and the thought that her grandparents came from this area and how cool it was to think that she lived on a ski hill in northern Canada and her grandparents came from a town with a ski hill in northern Iceland! Fate! This just had to be the right place!

Isabelle and George proceeded to check out a little church at the base of hill down from the ski hill. They spent a fair bit of time wandering through the graveyard inspecting the gravestones for familiar names and dates of supposed relatives. They found none and became frustrated. George noticed a car parked out in front of the church and they decided to go into the church to see if they could find anyone to chat with. Hopefully they would be able to speak English!

They did find a nice lady in the church who was very friendly and eager to help, and she spoke fluent English. She was excited to help and mentioned another couple of churches that had graveyards that could be explored. She mentioned that her son was an accomplished skier and had attended the Vancouver 2010 Olympics in Canada! Another sign of fate for sure! The woman left them to carry on with her business and Isabelle and George headed down in Dalvik to find some lunch.

They were walking along the street when the woman

from the church noticed them again and motioned them over to her car. She offered to drive to the other churches so they could follow her in their rental car. She also mentioned that they should try and look up the family historical information in the archives at the public library in Dalvik. Pleased with this source of hope, Isabelle and George followed her in their car to the other church and waved as she drove off once they were parked. Much more time was consumed as they wandered around the gravesite and took notice of the names and dates. Again, nothing was found at all to reference the family history.

Dismayed, Isabelle and George decided to head to the public library to check out the archives. There they met with a very charming lady who spent a great deal of time listening to their story and trying to sort out what she could about where the family might have been from. She shared with them that she had done some travelling and spent some time at the University of Northern British Columbia in Prince George researching information for the library. Wow! This was another connection to Canada and to the north where they were from. She soon determined that the family was not from Dalvik but that Dalabae was indeed the correct name. The woman knew of a colleague in Siglufjordur at the public library archives. It seemed that Dalabae was a farm in that area that wasn't really that far from Dalvik by car.

Before long, the woman had chatted with her colleague. The colleague exclaimed that she did know of Dalabae and in fact she knew the man that owned Dalabae! How exciting! It was arranged that Isabelle and George would drive immediately to Siglufjordur to the public library archives to meet with this man and the colleague. Nervously, Isabelle and George shook hands with the kind woman in Dalvik and headed out towards Siglufjordur. What an exciting day it had turned out to be! Perhaps they were getting somewhere with the research. The people they had met were so friendly and helpful. Anything was possible.

Within the hour, Isabelle and George had arrived in Siglufjordur at the public library archives and met the woman who waited for them. She spoke English and was very helpful. She was still trying to locate the marriage records in her books but was unable to do so. She did find an old book that contained a picture of the farmhouse at Dalabae with a story about the farm. It was all in Icelandic, but the picture was a treasure. Maybe one day someone in the family could read the Icelandic language. A tall lanky older man with a slightly shorter older woman entered the library and approached the desk. The woman introduced Isabelle and George to Siggi and Sika. Siggi was the owner of the farm called Dalabae. Johan and Gudrun were married at the farm her parents owned and it was called Dalabae. That was why no reference could be found in the records of a place called Dalabae. Siggi went on to state that he was the son of Gudrun's brother and therefore he was my cousin. At home, he had many pictures of Gudrun and her family and exclaimed to Isabelle that she looked just like Gudrun so he knew for sure that Isabelle was family! How incredible was that!

Siggi and Sika were lovely people and invited Isabelle and George back to their home. Tea and simple

Icelandic goodies were served and enjoyed, and many pictures were shared with the couple. Both Siggi and Sig spoke fluent English and spoke highly of their own children and grandchildren and a wish to visit Canada one day. Isabelle and George invited them to come to stay with them in British Columbia. Siggi shared with George a piece of the corbel off of the old farmhouse that was featured in the book that the woman at the library had given Isabelle. The old farmhouse had been dismantled and many pieces saved. As Isabelle was a granddaughter of Gudrun's, he wanted her to have a piece of the homestead. Tears slipped from Isabelle's eyes at the thoughtful gesture. How this piece of old wood and the still in-tack nails would fit in her suitcase back to Canada was a mystery, but she accepted the corbel with pleasure.

Siggi and Sika led them downstairs to put on tall rubber boots and the four of them headed off in Siggi's vehicle to go and see the homestead firsthand. What an incredible experience! The farm was situated on the edge of the Artic Ocean with the muskeg land looming upwards across the valley towards the towering mountains. They tramped across the muskeg and sunk every now and then. Isabelle's boots filled with water as they were full of holes! It was astounding to think that her roots began at this place and the hardships that occurred were unimaginable! The courage, tenacity and strength of the people and especially of the women were awe-inspiring. Isabelle came from amazingly hardworking people.

Siggi was a wealth of information on this history of the family. He knew of both Johan's and Gudrun's roots.

Johan and Gudrun grew up on neighbouring farms and were sweethearts. Both led hard lives on the farm but being much older, Johan had left home early and immigrated to Canada and returned again after some time to marry Gudrun and in the end to bring his mother, brother and nephew back to Canada with them.

There were, by Siggi's estimation, over one-hundred people living in and around the area north of Akureyri that they could count as family. Absolutely amazing that such success was found on this trip to Iceland. The results far exceeded any expectation of living relatives as it was believed that when Johan and Gudrun travelled to Canada that they brought with them all or nearly all of the remaining family they had. It is true that Gudrun's brother had travelled to Canada with them in 1913 but he did not like the country, and he returned to Iceland the year following.

Isabelle was excited and encouraged that she might be able to find equal success in locating relatives or faeries that might remember Poppy.

Time ran short and Isabelle and George had to conclude their journey to Iceland and return to Canada, but Isabelle was hopeful that they would return in a few years with Tux to celebrate his sixty-fifth birthday and to return Poppy to Iceland after more than one-hundred years in Canada to spend her final years in her homeland and to fulfill her commitment to the President. It was Poppy's turn to retire and get to know her own extended family and reconnect with those that would still remember her.

Chapter 10
Sunshine Coast, British Columbia,
Canada and Iceland

2016 – 2018

The long cold winters of Northern British Columbia were taking a toll on Poppy. She was spending more and more of her time cocooned in her wings and rarely came out for any occasion.

In their retirement, Isabelle and George rarely spent any time in Northern British Columbia and in the fall of 2017 decided to sell their beloved home at the ski hill. All personal items were packed up and moved to a home on the Sunshine Coast. The little slate house was moved as well and given the temperate climate at the new house, Poppy found that she could set up herself and live properly in her lovely little home. She was so pleased. It seemed as if new life had been breathed into Poppy and she so looked forward to each new day as she explored her surroundings. She too was enjoying her retirement as there were no children to care for and in place of a position of responsibility, Poppy took to learning all about the new flowers and animals that surrounded her little slate house.

The occasion of Tux's sixty-fifth birthday was rolling around and Isabelle and George began researching the upcoming holiday to Iceland. While they wanted to show Tux the wonders that they had experienced on their last visit, Isabelle and George wanted to ensure that Poppy would be well taken care on her return to Iceland.

It was a bittersweet day when Poppy tidied her little home for the very last time. She spent time setting all her possessions carefully as if someone might be living in her home. She said tearful goodbyes to her forest friends. Her slate home would become a haven for travelling animals as a place to rest and enjoy a meal. A small statue of a faery and garden gnome were placed at the doorway to ensure the safety and security of the sanctuary.

Poppy had tearful goodbyes with the family and prepared herself for the long journey. As airport security would be troublesome, it was imperative that Poppy incase herself in her wings to ensure a deep and lasting hibernation so that she would be safe within the large suitcase that Isabelle was taking to Iceland. Isabelle carefully placed a deeply sleeping Poppy within the long pocket at the back of the inside of the suitcase and ensured that soft socks and shirts protected Poppy from the danger of any movement of hard objects in the suitcase. It is well known that suitcases endure some pretty horrific jostling on the journey from the airport check-in to the airplane cargo area and off again once the airplane lands.

Isabelle and George along with Tux eagerly anticipated the travel from Vancouver to Iceland and enjoyed an uneventful flight. Isabelle was extremely worried about the length of the trip, the altitude effects on Poppy and the extreme cold temperature that Poppy would be exposed to. It was a complete unknown as to how the hibernating state that Poppy was in that would determine her resilience to the challenges of the flight.

Once the aircraft had landed, baggage was claimed and the trio were checked into their rental accommodation in Reykjavik, Isabelle anxiously unzipped the suitcase and reached into the back of the suitcase to gently lift out the wing encased faery. With shaking hands, Isabelle placed the small body between the pillows on the bed and began lightly stroking the soft, silky wings that held Poppy. For several minutes, Isabelle continued her gentle motions. Tears ran down Isabelle's checks as she choked back her sobs. Surely Poppy would be coming around by now. It never took long for Poppy to come out of her hibernating state if Isabelle needed to rouse her. Isabelle was wracked with guilt at the thought that the airplane ride had caused harm to Poppy. Poppy had arrived in Canada via water and really should have returned that way as well. In exhaustion, Isabelle lied down next to Poppy and fell into a troubled sleep.

"Ouch, owie, oh my that really hurts!" cried Poppy. "What is happening to me?" Poppy whimpered. Isabelle woke with a start and tried to gather Poppy in her hands. Poppy's wings had opened but Poppy was struggling to move without pain. Isabelle gently rubbed Poppy's limbs and soon Poppy quietened and was peaceful.

"Am I here?" a delighted Poppy questioned Isabelle. "Am I really here?"

The tingling of Poppy's limbs subsided, and she jumped up and ran along the top of the bed. "I feel wonderful now! "What happened to make me hurt do you think Isabelle?" pondered Poppy.

Before Isabelle could respond, George answered "We often times have limbs that seem to fall asleep and when we attempt to use them, they slowly come back to life and tingle a bit as the blood flows again to the parts of the limb that were somewhat starved of blood flow. Simple really. But it can be rather painful." George was always clever at explaining science things.

Thankfully, there were no harmful effects to Poppy as a result of the airplane flight. She was a good as ever. Here she was — back in Iceland — and she was one-hundred-and-twenty-four years old! My goodness! Such an age and she felt terrific! Her hair was changed little although it was somewhat thinner, still curly and her blonde colour sported many tinsel highlights that were attractive and gave her an aura of angelic beauty. Poppy laughed as she was joking around with Tux. "How is it that the Icelandic men and your little sister had lovely curls when they were young, and now, as you age, the curls disappear, and you are left with a thinning head of hair. And the Icelandic women end up with thick brown hair that simply turns to tinsel in their later years!" Isabelle turned to look at Tux's face at Poppy's observations, and was relieved to see that he took the comments in the good humour that was intended.

"Well, what wasn't fair when we were younger, turns out to be a blessing as we reach our later years. Good for us Icelandic women I say!" laughed Isabelle. Tux arched his head backwards and laughed heartily.

Tux was anxious to get on with exploring Iceland and

they were to be in and around Reykjavik for the next few days. They had a rental car and were able to get out and see the highlights of the southwestern part of Iceland. A small sac had been fashioned for Poppy, much like the sac that had been made for Poppy when she began to ride with Lizzie up the chairlift to experience the thrill of flying down the hill as Lizzie skied to the bottom.

Poppy was anxious to see Iceland with Tux's eyes and enthusiasm. Poppy had never been to this part of Iceland, in fact, she had never travelled outside of her home territory of Eyjafjordur Fjord in northern Iceland. It had been one-hundred-and-five years since she left Iceland and she was back in her own country. Poppy's eyes welled at the thought of going back to her home and finding any remaining friends or relatives. Poppy was very thankful to her adopted family for the opportunity to come home again. Love and enduring friendship were so precious.

Isabelle and George spent several days travelling about showing Tux and Poppy the sights and marveling at the wonders of Iceland. Tourism in Iceland has grown tremendously in recent years due to the magnificence of the natural wonders of the waterfalls, the volcanoes, the glaciers, the terrain and the oceans. The people of Iceland are genuinely kind and helpful and proud of their country and are happy to share the history with visitors.

Isabelle had researched hidden peoples and had some ideas of where they might find answers to locate the relatives of Poppy. On their last trip to Iceland, Isabelle and George had spotted several places where houses of hidden peoples were identified for travelers. They would be driving by the area on the way to Akureyri and hoped to stop and check out any information they could gather on hidden peoples of today. There was also a story printed about the recently disturbed dwelling of hidden peoples just north of Siglufjordur that was worth checking out. After all, this was near the area that young Hjortur came from in 1913 and if there are hidden peoples there now, then perhaps information would be available to assist in getting Poppy reunited with her family.

Isabelle had also discovered that Alfaborg is a city of the hidden people in Borgarfjordur-Eystri in East Iceland not necessarily close to where Poppy came from, but it is where the manor of the highest ranking of the hidden people is. It is believed that the Queen of the Hidden People resides in Alfaborg!

Finally, it was time for the travelers to leave Reykjavik and make their way along the circle road up towards Akureyri. Poppy was experiencing some tummy problems due to the anxiety of the unknown and her nervousness was affecting the others. Poppy was constantly asking George to pull over with the car so that she could walk a little and take deep breaths of the cool Icelandic air. She marveled at the landscape and it took forever to go even a short distance along their journey. They stopped for a coffee and a bathroom break in Borgarnes and it was when they were about a half hour outside of this little town that Poppy exclaimed "Stop, oh please stop!" An overwhelming sense of familiarity flowed into Poppy and she was beside herself with anticipation. "I, I have to get out. Please. Wait here. I just have to look around. I don't know how to explain it but I must get out and look around."

George slowed the car and found an easy spot to pull off on the side of the road and Poppy hurriedly bundled herself up. Isabelle lifted Poppy up and placed her on the ground a safe distance from the road and the car. Poppy took off running up the hillside and disappeared behind a grouping of rocks. George and Tux took the opportunity to take some awesome shots of the rolling hills and sparse vegetation with the meandering river as a backdrop. Isabelle waited patiently beside the car her eyes peeled for any movement from behind the rocks. It seemed to take forever, but Poppy eventually popped her head out and came running back to Isabelle at full speed! "I simply can't believe it! I can't! I really spoke to a faery! She has so much to share with me. She was shy of me at first but she had to agree that I do look just like her! "I need to go back and spend some time with her and she is going to take me to visit her family. She has a very old grandmother who might be able to help me out. Please say I can go back and visit with her! Please! Please!" Isabelle was fretful and anxious about letting Poppy out of her sight but she certainly understood the need for Poppy to get more information from her new friend. That was the purpose of this trip after all, to find Poppy's family and get her back to her roots. And for Tux of course!

Isabelle and George had a quick discussion and decided that they would give Poppy some time to learn what she could from the grandmother of her new friend. Poppy was ecstatic and ran off again up behind the rocks with a promise to return in a few hours. George, Tux and Isabelle spent their time hiking around the area. Isabelle headed back to the car and grabbed the pack sack and looked around for a spot to sit and enjoy the sights. She had just begun setting out a picnic lunch when the men appeared and they all sat and enjoyed a simple lunch of cold hard-boiled eggs, thin sliced dense bread and pickled beets! They washed their lunch down with bottles of water and then reached for the treat of the day, assorted licorice candies. Tux was not at all enamored with the licorice treats so he enjoyed some chocolate candies without the licorice flavouring!

Poppy returned within the allotted time and was beaming from ear to ear. Her nervous stomach had disappeared, and she was left was a buzzing excitement that was obvious to all of those around her. She had so much so share with the others and could hardly contain herself.

Isabelle soothed her "Poppy. Breathe. Slow down a little. We can hardly understand you. You are speaking way too fast for us to understand you."

Poppy took gulping breaths and started again. "I met the grandmother of my friend. She remembers the time when all of the young faeries were called to help the country's young people in crisis! She remembers!" Poppy started to cry softly in her hands.

"Oh Poppy!" Isabelle gathered Poppy up in her arms and cuddled her close. "Start at the beginning. Tell us what you found out."

Poppy stirred in Isabelle's embrace and began to tell the story. "It really is as I remembered as a young faery.

My memory is still just as great as it always was. It was Queen Hildur and the President Hannes Halfstein of Iceland that made the decree that the young faeries were to assist the young children of the country who were in distress. The grandmother could hardly believe that I had provided such a long service to the family and that I had actually left the country. That was never the intent. I could have chosen not to go with the Hjortur's family when I did. I could have stayed here. I could have found another child to befriend." Poppy began to sob. "I could have married and had children of my own. What is to become of me now?" she asked through teary eyes.

Isabelle hugged Poppy tighter and responded "We are forever grateful for the friendship and mentoring that you have provided the children of our family. We will do everything we can to help you find your family and if we can't, you may choose to return to Canada with us. We are your family too. We love and appreciate you so very much." Isabelle murmured to Poppy while trying to soothe her broken heart. Soon Poppy's tears subsided and she wiped her face.

"I am ready to continue our journey. The grandmother told me that many faeries continued to live in and around their original homes in the outcroppings of rocks in the mountains. I want to try and find my family. I want to see who is left. Perhaps I have nieces and nephews to love." Poppy sniffed and held her handkerchief to her dripping nose.

George started up the car and they began again on their journey to Akureyri marveling at the landscape along with the way. Poppy was quiet on the journey whereas Tux and Isabelle chatted excitedly along the way as Isabelle and George pointed out certain points of interest to Tux. It was a beautiful day with scattered clouds. Bits of sunshine popped out of the clouds highlighting the rocky terrain. Isabelle wondered how many hidden peoples lived among the rock outcroppings. What seemed so barren may have been filled with other life forms. It really was a wondrous place this Iceland.

Once they arrived in Akureyri, Isabelle entered the address of the rental accommodation into the GPS system and before long they were parked in front of their home for the next week. Isabelle spied a woman coming out of a doorway on the second floor, so she quickly exited the car and ran up to the woman. The woman happened to be the cleaner and she was able to grant them access to the house and showed Isabelle around the small apartment. It would suit them all just fine and best of all, they were only an hour or so away from Siglufjordur. They all unloaded the car and Isabelle made up a little area for Poppy in the deep windowsill in Isabelle and George's bedroom. The window looked out over the yard and onto the road. Isabelle found a long wooden bowl in the kitchen and lined it with hand towels and then placed the large handkerchiefs that Poppy so loved on top of the towels and tucked it in to form the base of a mattress and sheet. A second handkerchief was placed on top and then a small scarf completed the bedding. There was a school across from the house and Poppy enjoyed sitting in her cozy bed while leaning onto the window with her head nestled into her hands. She would gaze out at the children playing and daydream about what she might find when and if she found her family. Poppy alternated between being very anxious and being very optimistic about having nieces and nephews.

Plans were made to explore the area for the next few days and Isabelle arranged with Cousin Siggi to meet Tux so that he could meet the extended family and perhaps see the original homesteads where their grandmother and grandfather lived as children.

The weather had turned dismal, and the rain pelted the windshield as George drove out along the fjord to Dalvik. While Poppy was anxious to find her family, the other purpose of the travel to Iceland was for Tux to explore and learn about the country. A stop in Dalvik to a whale watching business was on the agenda and they were able to secure tickets for a whale watching tour that very afternoon. Tux was very pleased but nervous. Water was not something he was comfortable with, but he really wanted to see the whales and to fish off the boat as had been promised. Another picnic lunch was enjoyed and then it was time to head over for the boat tour.

Poppy was again placed in the little sac to ensure her warmth and safety and they all spent an enjoyable afternoon cruising up and down the fjord as the vessel maneuvered to be at the ready for the whales as they breached out of the water. It was simply amazing! Such large, graceful beasts! For several hours the vessel motored along with many of the passengers getting some amazing photographs of the whales. Finally, it was time to head closer in. The boat was slowed and the tour guide prepared fishing rods for many people and they in turn would share their rod once they had caught a fish.

Tux was ecstatic as he caught the first and the largest fish of any of the passengers! Each fish was placed in a plastic bin and on the way back to the harbour, the tour guide expertly filleted all of the fish. Once back at the whale-watching base, the tour guide barbecued the catch and each of the passengers sampled the delicious fish! It was an incredible afternoon, and a big grin was evident on Tux's face.

The day was beginning to darken and while the rain had held off somewhat for the boat tour, it was now back on to a downpour. It was time to head back to the apartment for a cozy evening inside reminiscing about the day's adventures.

The next day didn't fare any better with the weather but visiting was on the agenda for the day and George drove out past Dalvik along the fjord and through tunnels in the mountains to get to Cousin Siggi's house in Siglufjordur. Tux was in awe by the tunnels, but Poppy was terrified. She did not like being inside the rock for such a long distance. The first of the tunnels was a one-way tunnel that was a challenge for the driver as you had to pay close attention to oncoming traffic and poke into a small space chiseled into the rock to avoid a collision! These small spaces were placed at intervals along the tunnel to allow for two-way traffic. The one-way tunnel was built in 1967 and prior to then access in and out of Siglufjordur during the winter months was determined on the snow load and weather conditions of the day. The two-way tunnel between Siglufjordur and Olafsfjordur was built in 2010.

Tux and George were impressed by the engineering

and began to chat about the benefits and technology. Poppy groaned in dismay and hid her face in her hands to avoid looking about. The pelting rain announced to the occupants of the car that they had exited the tunnel.

It wasn't much further to Cousin Siggi's house, so Isabelle prepared Poppy for a rest in the cocoon of her wings. It had been decided that since not all Icelanders believe in hidden peoples nor faeries and that the relationship with Cousin Siggi was very fresh and new, Isabelle had chosen not to disclose to Cousin Siggi that Poppy existed and that they were also in Iceland to try and reunite Poppy with her family. That part of the trip to Iceland would remain a private matter. There was no intent to bring insult to Cousin Siggi and Isabelle was determined not to lose the respect or friendship of this newly found family.

Isabelle and George introduced Tux to Cousin Siggi and his wife and there was an immediate connection between Tux and Siggi. The two of them hit it off and were soon deep in conversation with Siggi showing Tux numerous pieces of family history in the form of pictures, documents, paintings and artifacts. Cousin Siggi's wife prepared a wonderful Icelandic spread of sweet and savory goodies along with coffee and tea. Once they had filled up on the goodies, they headed downstairs to put on tall gumboots and followed Cousin Siggi and his wife out to the vehicles.

George followed a short distance behind their car. Tux rode with Siggi as the two had still not stopped chatting about this and that. Isabelle did not disturb Poppy as she was resting in her cocoon, and they were not done visiting. George kept pace with Cousin Siggi and soon they were gazing down upon the land of the homestead.

Isabelle felt the tears begin to form again. She had first laid eyes upon this beautiful setting a few years before, when they had visited, and here she was again, with the privilege of walking the land. It was a very harsh land sitting upon the edge of the Artic Ocean with the waves lapping and splashing up on the rocky banks. The land was uneven and was difficult to walk upon. It was a marsh hence the need for the tall rubber boots. While it seemed at a distance to be a lovely pasture of gently swaying grasses, it was a lumpy, oozing bed of spongy mosses and decaying plant matter. It was a wetland. The land was suitable for sheep farming but little else. It was evident that no crops or vegetables had ever been grown on this desolate piece of land.

A small driveway appeared, and George parked beside Cousin Siggi and they all spent some time walking out and along the land. Cousin Siggi walked out towards to the location of the original home, and they stood in awe. How on earth could a family have lived on such land and made a living? It was true that the views and the vista were incredibly beautiful, but this was a harsh land. The Artic Ocean was at their feet with the slopes of the mountains at their back. Isabelle was filled with amazement that her great-grandmother had actually packed each piece of lumber for the homestead from the shores of the Artic Ocean and up to the building site. The lumber had been shipped directly from Norway to the site. Goodness, it was awkward to just walk along the land never mind carrying pieces of lumber.

Isabelle's heritage was of tough stock. The women were strong. The men were strong. They were doers. They were survivors. And Poppy was right along there in spirit. She had the qualities of this Icelandic heritage - she never gave up on her assignment to the family and carried on providing her service and left her family and her country because it was in her mind the right thing to do. Tux stood in disbelief. Cousin Siggi stood proudly.

Isabelle was blessed to find and reconnect with her heritage. She simply must see that Poppy had that same opportunity. She had to get Poppy back to her family. Just prior to the one-way tunnel that they had travelled through to come to the homestead, Isabelle had noticed the very large boulder that was sitting at the side of highway. She recognized this from the newspaper article that she had found online while researching for some ideas on where to find hidden peoples in Iceland. It seems that dirt had been dumped on a rock during road construction. The heavy rains in the summer season had perhaps caused mudslides. The locals had suspected that it was elves that had caused the mudslides as the rock had a special name in Icelandic folklore "Alfkonusteinn"." Isabelle wondered if perhaps they might find some information about hidden people and faeries around this area.

If Poppy had experienced a deep sense of knowing on the drive to Akureyri that caused her to want to stop and check out a rock outcropping, then perhaps they could look into this bolder. Another piece that gave Isabelle hope was that the area around the fjord of

Siglufjordur was called Trollaskagi. Trollaskagi is a peninsula northwest of Akureyri and the name means "peninsula of the trolls"." Could this be a sign of hidden peoples nearby?

After walking the property, they got in the vehicles and followed Siggi as he drove further along the road to a viewpoint that looked down upon another homestead that was separated from the family's homestead by a creek meandering from the base of the mountain and across the muskeg to the ocean below. Siggi explained that the homestead closest to them now, once belonged to their grandfather's family! Imagine both of their grandparents living next door to one another as children! It seems that they fell in love as teenagers and their grandfather moved away to Canada in 1905 to begin a new life. He returned after his father died. He arrived back in Iceland in 1912 and married his sweetheart and returned to Canada with his family and the promise of a bright future. While the romance was wonderful, the struggles were real, and it was at this time that Poppy came into the picture to begin her life with their family. Time to get on with finding Poppy's family for her to return home.

They visited the rest of the afternoon with Cousin Siggi and his wife and then said their goodbyes. They were thrilled with their visit but anxious to begin their search. The light of the day was beginning to fade so they made their way back to Akureyri and did not stop to explore the big boulder. Isabelle roused Poppy from her cocoon and Poppy took some time to regain her energy. Isabelle worried that Poppy was beginning to become depressed and upset at the passage of time. What if Poppy's family could not be found? Anxiety was evident for both Isabelle and Poppy. They both slept fitfully and woke the next day feeling rather sluggish. Would today be the day that Poppy was reunited with her family?

It was decided that an early start was best in the morning. The weather was co-operating. It was bright and sunny. It was a promising start to the day. George drove along the fjord northwest of Akureyri and back along the tunnels towards Siglufjordur. Once they were past the town itself, Isabelle noticed the big boulder as they were coming up on the right alongside the road and looking down the rocky bank to the water below.

A small pullout allowed George to park the car safely on the side of the road. George and Tux got out of the car for some photo opportunities and Isabelle bundled Poppy up and carried her out of the car and up towards the boulder. A great energy began to emerge from Poppy.

"Quickly, quickly!" Poppy whispered to Isabelle. "I feel so very strange, but excited at the same time! What on earth is happening to me? Poppy exclaimed. "Let me down please!" pleaded Poppy. Isabelle bent and placed Poppy on the ground and Poppy turned and looked up at Isabelle. "I must go and explore. Wait for me. Please." Poppy begged of Isabelle.

"Of course, Poppy. That is why we are here. We will be right here waiting for you. But please come back if you find out anything. We need to know that you are safe. We will be right here," Isabelle responded in a soft, caring voice. "You go and explore!" Isabelle watched Poppy run off and wiped the tears from her face. "Please let her find out some information on her family!" prayed Isabelle.

A great deal of time passed and soon it was late afternoon. George and Tux and Isabelle had brought a few snacks with them and some bottles of water, but they were hungry and stiff from sitting on the edge of the road, just waiting patiently. Isabelle nodded off and was awakened by the loud sound of Poppy screeching at the top of her lungs. "I have a family, I have a family! I can't believe it! I really do have my own family!" and then Poppy burst into tears. Isabelle gathered Poppy in her arms and held her close.

"Tell us, everything. Slow down. Start at the beginning and tell us what you have been up to for, oh my goodness, the past six hours!" Isabelle exclaimed.

Poppy took gulps of air and began to tell what she had learned while visiting the hidden people of the boulder.

Poppy met an older man who knew her family well. There were certainly a good many of her family left in the area. Poppy had grown up in the mountains just up from the family homestead where she had been placed in her very first assignment as a mentoring faery. Jon, the huldofolk man that shared the information about her family with Poppy, relayed the fact that her family members still lived up in the mountains and he could show Poppy where they lived. Poppy had explained to Jon that she had travelled to Canada and lived there for all of these years, but that she had been returned to Iceland by that same family and they wished to take her to her family. Jon agreed that this was the best and arranged to meet them at the Isabelle's family homestead at the base of the mountain in a day's time.

Jon had suggested that the humans travel by horse up the mountain as it was a very long journey and that they were unlikely to be successful in a climb. He worried too that Poppy was unused to such a climb and suggested that both she and him travel up on the horse with Isabelle.

Isabelle, George and Tux discussed this plan of Poppy's and Jon's and decided that it made good sense. Poppy hopped down and returned to the boulder to seek out Jon and let him know that they would meet him at the homestead the following day. Isabelle and George needed to make arrangements for a horse tour up the mountain. There was much to do.

When Poppy had returned, George turned and pointed the car towards the homestead. He explained that they would be travelling to Hofsos right away to enjoy the infinity pool with the magnificent views of the fjord and enjoy a meal. They would then make arrangements for a small group horseback riding tour of the mountain above the homestead. Isabelle had previously researched the horseback riding tour companies around Akureyri and had found this one particularly interesting. The only drawback was that they recommended riders to be experienced. While Isabelle and George had limited experience on a horse, Tux was not at all comfortable on a horse. Riding an Icelandic horse in Iceland was definitely on Isabelle's bucket list and she was game. If Tux were too uncomfortable on a horse, then he would stay behind while George and Isabelle took Poppy and Jon on this journey.

It wasn't too long before they were in Hofsos enjoying an evening meal. All of them were famished and ate a hearty meal. Poppy was anxious again and barely touched her meal.

Isabelle looked over at her worriedly and wondered how the day would go tomorrow. George contacted the horseback riding tour company and arrangements were made for the three of them to have a tour first thing in the morning.

They then made their way to the pool at Hofsos and were amazed at the stunning views of the fjord while they soaked away their achy muscles. Soon they were dried and back in the car for the long drive back to Akureyri. It would be a long day tomorrow and they needed to get a good sleep. George was the only person in the vehicle who was able to stay awake for the drive home. The others succumbed to their relaxed state brought on by the calming waters of the infinity pool. It was a wonderful last evening with Poppy, or so they hoped.

Early the next morning, all of Poppy's belongings were packed into a small satchel and she buzzed about with excitement and anticipation. They all dressed warmly as the mountains would be cool. George drove to the horseback riding stables and parked the car. Once the trio was dressed in the warm, one-piece coveralls and had helmets fastened, an orientation was performed and then they were able to set off.

Tux froze once up on the horse and immediately wanted to get off. George began to soothe Tux but the young horsewoman intervened and soon had Tux relaxed and a little more confident as he sat on his horse while listening to the encouragement from the young woman. Tux was smitten and was not about to get off his horse.

Isabelle had Poppy tucked safely in her coverall breast pocket and Poppy was able to stand up and keep an eye on her surroundings. George and Tux wanted to take some photographs but the horsewoman was adamant that the group stay together at all times.

Safety was a huge priority.

They started off from the stables and made their way along the side of the road and across the muskeg of the properties that they passed through. It was a beautiful ride. The day was bright and sunny again and the views were breathtaking as they made their way along the road to the point of the ascent of the mountain. The ride up to the point of the base of the mountain was especially easy for all of them and even Tux was beginning to relax and enjoy himself. They stopped at the base of the mountain and dismounted. The horses were tethered to allow them to graze on the scrub grasses before their grueling journey ahead. The horses were typical of the Icelandic breeds.

Somehow or other Tux had been given the tallest, most majestic horse with a long flowing mane. He had a gentle manner and listened well. The horse was quite used to being a tour guide. George had a much smaller horse and would have preferred to have ridden the horse that Tux had. George's horse had gentle manner as well. Isabelle would have liked a horse with the girly-fringed mane and bangs but was given a petite horse with a short mane and a lazy manner. This horse preferred to sway back and forth while sashaying along the path. Isabelle wondered how the horse would do on the incline up the mountain.

While the group waited for the horses to rest at the base of the mountain, Poppy gently nudged Isabelle and pointed towards an outcropping of rocks where Poppy had spied Jon waiting patiently for them to arrive. Isabelle quietly motioned for George to fetch Jon.

Introductions were made by Poppy and soon Jon was tucked inside the other breast pocket of Isabelle's coveralls.

The horsewoman instructed the riders to remount and soon the group was off and up the mountain on the next part of their trek. The horsewoman had no idea that there was a purpose to this tour and kept the group entertained with information about the area and the inhabitants and history. The horses expertly negotiated the narrow trails picking their way between stones and roots along the path. This was the route that Isabelle and Tux's ancestors had travelled before the tunnels and roads were in place as they were today.

Poppy was entranced at the scenery and the smells. She was so looking forward to the arrival at her home. Jon pointed out various homes of faeries and hidden peoples and Isabelle was simply amazed at the number of places that they inhabited. She had no idea that there were so many hidden peoples living in this area of Northern Iceland. The day passed slowly as the group made their way up the mountain.

By late afternoon, the sun was beginning to fade and the group was tiring. The trek was exhausting and none of them were used to sitting in the saddle for so many hours. Isabelle wished her horse would stop with the hip swaying side to side. The horsewoman pointed out the sheep grazing along the way and Isabelle loved to see the sheep barely glancing up as the horses wandered by on their way. The animals simply acknowledged one another and went on with their business. None of the animals felt threatened by the presence of the humans on horseback.

The horsewoman decided it was time for a break as she wanted to check the area to see if it would be a suitable spot for a camp spot for the night. While Isabelle wanted dearly to get off the horse, she wasn't so sure she wanted to sleep on the ground in a sleeping bag. The advertisement for this horseback-riding trek had promised open air sleeping as the Northern Lights were expected to be tremendous. While the Northern Lights were certainly something that they looked forward to, getting Poppy settled with her family was the first priority.

While the horsewoman began her exploration of a suitable spot, Jon whispered to Poppy and Isabelle that Poppy's family was located just a short distance away and that this would indeed be a great spot to stop for the night. George called out to the horsewoman that he felt this would be a good spot given the terrific views down onto the homestead and out to the Artic Ocean. A little higher up and over and you could see down to the valley leading into Siglufjordur. If they kept to this side of the mountain, they would be protected from the winds and could look down on their history. And Poppy would be close to home.

While the horsewoman arranged the camp set up with the help of George and Tux, the horses were tethered and allowed to graze and relax. Soon the camp kitchen was ready and a fire was lit to cook a simple meal. George, Tux and Isabelle were simply starving and would have eaten just about anything.

Jon had gone off by himself and returned just a little while later with an older faery. He walked with a cane and he was bent with age. His facial features were covered by the masses of white hair of his beard and his full head of hair. He walked with purpose and approached Isabelle. She bent down and placed Poppy on the ground. All was very quiet. George and Tux turned to look at what was happening.

The old faery approached Poppy. He took a very close look at her and gazed deeply into her eyes. Poppy began to tremble. The old faery spoke softly "I cannot believe my eyes. It is my youngest child returned to me. I prayed for this day for so long but did not really believe I would ever see you again." He began to sob. He held out his arms wide. Poppy ran into his arms and he held her tight in his hug.

"Pops! Oh Pops! I never believed that you would still be of this earth! I have missed you so! I thought I might have some nieces and nephews, but I never believed I would find you!" Poppy cried as he tightened her in his hold. Jon stood quietly aside.

The old faery loosened his hold and turned to Isabelle and George and Tux. "Thank you so very much for returning my darling daughter to me. I have known deep in my heart that she was well and happy and I knew that she would one day return to me. I have had faith," the old faery exclaimed. "There are a very many family members that will be anxious to see Poppy, to get to know her again. She left home at such an early age and we believe that she may have been the only faery to take her responsibilities so seriously that she travelled to another country to serve a family. We have all prayed for this day," the old faery said.

Poppy beamed up at Isabelle. Tears shone on her face, tears of happiness and joy. "You were right Isabelle. My family is here. I am home. I am so thankful that you brought me home!" Poppy whispered to Isabelle.

"We didn't bring you all this way to stand here and say goodbye for a long time! Give us all a hug. We offer the best of wishes to you and all of your family. Our family cannot thank you enough for the service and friendship you have given us all. We love you, Poppy!" Isabelle gathered Poppy in her arms and gave her a big hug and wiped the tears from Poppy's face. George gathered Poppy in his arms and hugged her tight. Tux gave Poppy a huge hug. Tears were flowing freely for all of them. Jon and Poppy and the old faery headed out arm in arm into the gentle scrub grasses and disappeared into the outcroppings of rock. Just like that and Poppy was gone. Isabelle began to sob.

George and Tux gathered Isabelle close, and they had a tight group hug. The horsewoman returned from gathering wood and wondered what on earth was going on with all of the crying. Isabelle just blubbered something about being sore and thankful at the same time for the opportunity for this ride.

Dinner was soon ready and they ate every morsel. They washed their meal down with a strong tea and laid down on their sleeping bags. It was beginning to cool down and Isabelle was tired of wearing the heavy coveralls, so she took them off and donned a sweatshirt instead and crawled inside the sleeping bag.

A strong desire to sleep overtook her and she was soon sleeping soundly.

A kaleidoscope of colour burst across the sky. Isabelle believed herself to be dreaming. George shook her awake. "Hey sleepyhead. Wake up. Look at that! This is just amazing! Isabelle sat up quickly. Tux roused himself awake as well. The sky exploded with colour. It was as if a band was playing a great tune and the lights and colours were dancing along to the beat. It was magical. It was heavenly. Isabelle lay back on her sleeping bag and kept her gaze on the sky. The colours were intense. The movement was spectacular. The sense of a world so powerful, so full of purpose was heavy on her heart. Isabelle could feel the presence of her father Svienne and her sister LeeBones. Isabelle wept for the beauty of the experience of the Northern Lights and the sense of sharing them here in this very special place with her loved ones gone from this earth. Poppy was home and she was loved, not forgotten.

Isabelle felt peace within her heart and in her soul. Thank you for sharing of yourself and for your kindness.

The End

Be Thankful

Be thankful that you don't already have everything you desire, If you did, what would there be to look forward to?

Be thankful when you don't know something For it gives you the opportunity to learn.

Be thankful for the difficult times. During those times you grow.

Be thankful for your limitations

Because they give you opportunities for improvement.

Be thankful for each new challenge Because it will build your strength and character.

Be thankful for your mistakes They will teach you valuable lessons.

Be thankful when you're tired and weary Because it means you've made a difference.

It is easy to be thankful for the good things.

A life of rich fulfillment comes to those who are also thankful for the setbacks.

GRATITUDE can turn a negative into a positive.

Find a way to be thankful for your troubles and they can become your blessings.

Author Unknown

Printed in the USA
CPSIA information can be obtained
at www.ICGtesting.com
JSHW080238131223
53709JS00002B/87